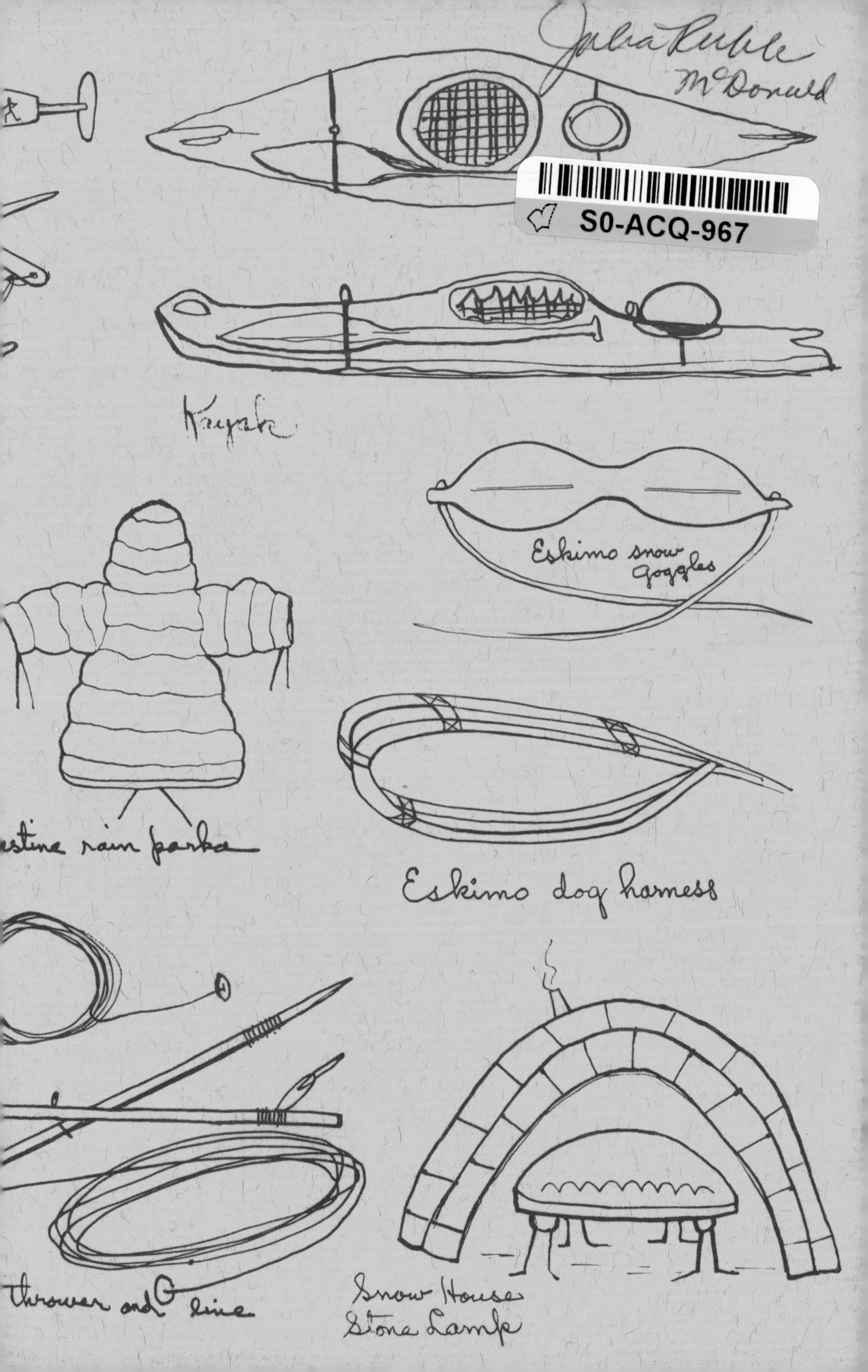
Kayak
Eskimo snow goggles
rain parka
Eskimo dog harness
thrower and line
Snow House
Stone Lamp

Shadows from the Singing House

Shadows from the Singing House

ESKIMO FOLK TALES

retold by Helen Caswell

illustrations by Robert Mayokok

Rutland . Vermont : Tokyo . Japan

CHARLES E. TUTTLE COMPANY

Poems included in the Prologue, "Sedna, the Sea Goddess," and "How the Guillemots Came" are taken from Knud Rasmussen's *Intellectual Culture of the Iglulik Eskimos* and are hereby reprinted by permission of the author's estate.

REPRESENTATIVES

For Continental Europe:
Boxerbooks, Inc., *Zurich*

For the British Isles:
Prentice-Hall International, Inc., *London*

For Australasia:
Paul Flesch & Co., Pty. Ltd., *Melbourne*

For Canada:
m. g. hurtig ltd., *Edmonton*

Published by the Charles E. Tuttle Company, Inc.
of Rutland, Vermont & Tokyo, Japan
with editorial offices at
Suido 1-chome, 2-6, Bunkyo-ku, Tokyo

Library of Congress Catalog Card No. 68-13867

First printing, 1968

Book design & typography: F. Sakade
PRINTED IN JAPAN

For Dwight
whose idea it was
and Maree
who may some day want to read it
to Sam

Table of Contents

IN THE SINGING HOUSE *the firelight makes shadows dance behind the storyteller's head. Sometimes they appear to have lives of their own, these shadows. It is easy to half close one's eyes and see ravens and dragons and the people of other times and other villages. The storyteller's voice goes on and on, like the voice of the sea, rising and falling, whispering and thundering. Night after night, the storyteller sings his shadowy tales.*

How else would the people know of all that has gone before?

Prologue

One should welcome the morning with these words:

> I arise from my couch
> With the morning song of the gray gull
> I arise from my couch
> With the morning song to look towards the dark
> I turn my glance towards the day.

These are magic words for mornings, very old, having come from ancient times through many grandfathers and grandmothers. For when people have grown old, and it is time for the soul to pass over into another existence, then words are the finest treasure, the only real treasure, that can be left to the young. And since the Eskimo has no way of writing his words, as the white man does, the words must be learned by heart. Thus the old people teach to the young the wisdom of their forefathers.

When the autumn is over and *Okeok*, the winter, has come, then the long night begins. The hard winds blow against the blocks of trampled snow that form the igloo walls, and drive the fresh snow against the thin skin of the window. Inside, the family sit together on the furs that cover the packed snow of the sleeping ledge. In the quiet closeness of the family, in the seal oil lamps' pale yellow light that glistens on the dripping ice of the vaulted walls, there is time to think of many mysterious things.

One thinks of *Inusia*, the soul—that small Eskimo-shape that lives within a bubble in the lower part of the body and does the breathing. It is the soul that gives beauty and purpose; it is what makes one a man and another a caribou or bear. When the hair is cut, part of the soul is cut away too, and when a man sleeps, *Inusia* hangs upside down by one big toe, almost ready to fall—death and sleep being very close.

One thinks of things like that, and one thinks also of the spirits that walk the hills and cry in the storm. There are so many spirits—the good *Ooleooyenuk*, who eats seaweed; the healer *Koopvilloorkju*, with his orange hair; *Toodlanak*, who drives deer close for the people to hunt; *Ataksak,* like a bright ball, who gives joy; the *Oyakkert,* who live in small stones and do nothing at all. And there are the *Akktonakjuvoonga* who live in the sea where some cry out "I am a rope" and others answer "Thou art a rope," but no one knows why.

One thinks of such things in the long night; one considers the many customs that have come down to these times from the ancient times. There are more customs even than there are spirits. During the long night one may play "cat's cradle," but when the sun is visible the "ring and pin" game may be played instead. After sneezing one must always say "*cacq*" to insure long life. And after the long night, when the sun first appears, children must run into the igloos and put out the lamps, so that new lights may be lit to greet the sun.

How did the customs begin? How did everything begin in ancient times? No one knows. Some say that in the beginning two men came down from the heavens, and one became a woman so that children could be born. Some say that the first children came up out of the ground and the first woman, going about with baby clothes, found them in the clumps of willows and dressed them. They say that when there were so many people that they needed dog teams, the first men went out with harnesses and stamped on the ground, saying, "*Hoc! Hoc! Hoc!*" and the first dogs came up out of the ground and shook the sand from their coats. In the same way, when the first men wanted some caribou, they dug a big hole in the earth and when enough caribou had come up through it they covered it over.

Such things are not to be understood. They simply must be believed, and the customs observed, in order to hold the world up and keep the spirits contented. Too many questions, too many thoughts about the hidden things will take away one's peaceful mind.

Life is a different matter when *Opingrak,* the spring, arrives. Then the rocks below the snow grow warm and the snow begins to melt. Everywhere is heard the trickling of water beneath the snow, and the air is not so cold, and the light comes—from no one point in particular but from everywhere. The ptarmigan and snow buntings appear, as do ducks at the edge of the ice. The seals come out of the water to sun themselves, and the walrus roars and whistles. The covering of white disappears and there is the yellow of poppies and buttercups, the blues and purples and reds and greens of lichen, rock rose and saxifrage, reindeer moss, blueberry, willow, and cotton grass. Beneath the sleeping ledge is the sound of running water and the scratch-scratch of the little lemming as he forages for moss beneath the snow.

Now summer comes and with it the hunting and fishing and the many tasks of preparing food for the winter. There is no time for thinking of the mysteries of life; there is only life and the living of it.

Then the northern lights begin to swing through the skies—and these are caused by spirits in the heavens, the "ballplayers," playing catch with a walrus head—when the northern lights leap in the skies, then autumn has come, and with autumn, the contests in the singing house.

All year the men have been thinking of their songs; they have been practicing them in secret. Now everyone files into the singing house, larger than the other houses, with a central pillar on which are fixed seal oil lamps. The leader takes his place near the center and the people seat themselves in circles against the walls, the men on one side and the women on the other.

First come the *okalugtuat,* the ancient songs. These tell the history of the people, and if the singer makes a mistake, the old people correct him. In this way the old songs stay the same, through the many years that lie between the ancient people and those alive today, and in spite of the many miles that separate the different villages.

After the *okalugtuat* come the *okalualarutit,* newer songs, perhaps only several hundred years old, or less. After this are the newest songs that have just been written this year. The time has come for each man to perform his song for the people.

The singer bends forward a little, swaying at the hips, rising up and sinking down from the knees, to a rhythm that he beats out on his drum. The *gilaut*, "that with which the spirits are called," is more like a tambourine than a drum, and is made of skin. The singer beats it more and more rapidly, his up-and-down movement more pronounced, while his wife leads the chorus in the women's section. It is a long, long song; it goes on for an hour, with the same tune, just a few notes repeated. Sometimes there are strange buzzing noises in it, and animal sounds, and the chorus that occurs again and again: *aja, aja—haja, haja.* And all the time the singer's eyes are closed, for he must look inside himself for his song.

Each man sings his own song, hoping that it will be such a good song that it will become one of the *okalualarutit*, to be sung by his children and their children and grandchildren.

This has been the way of things for a thousand years and more, though things are changing now. Everywhere in the world things are changing, and even for the Eskimo there are the changes of the white man's civilization that is coming closer to him. Only in the most distant places do men any longer cut squares of trampled snow and build their round houses, and there are guns to use now as well as harpoons, and many boats have motors. Although every man tries still to keep a peaceful mind it becomes more and more difficult, for life is more complicated now. There are more people, and more things, and the spirits are not as likely to come to men in such a life.

The Spirit of the Moon

IT IS THE SPIRIT of the Moon who supplies the people with children, and sets the currents of the sea in motion, and it is he to whom small boys look for guidance and the power of becoming good hunters. When the New Moon appears, the boys run out and find a patch of clean snow and there they place bowls of snow as offerings to the seals, and they call up to the Moon, "Give us luck in hunting!"

When people have grown very old and can no longer be of any use, and life has become heavier than death, it is the Spirit of the Moon who calls out to them, "Come to me! It is not painful to die; it is only a moment of dizziness. Come to me!"

In ancient times, the Moon and the Sun were brother

and sister. During one long night they were playing, running out-of-doors with lighted torches. The brother stumbled and fell, and the flame of his torch went out, so that it only glowed. His sister's torch continued to burn brightly. At this moment, they felt themselves rising into heaven, and so they came up into the sky, where they now have a house divided into two rooms.

During the summer, the Sun never goes inside; she is always out-of-doors, and the heat of her flaming torch melts the snow and makes the flowers grow. During this time, the Moon stays indoors all of the time.

When winter comes, the Sun goes inside and stays there, and the Moon has to supply light for the people. This is hard for him, since he has only a glowing torch that gives off no heat. Also, he has many other duties to attend to, and must sometimes disappear. When the moon is gone from his place in the sky, he is bringing seals around for the people to catch, or bringing souls to earth or taking them up to his house, since this is another of his tasks.

There was once a woman who made a visit to the Moon. This woman was unhappy because she had no children, and also because her husband was unkind to her, so she ran away to the hills. On her way, she saw a sled flying through the air and knew at once that the person riding on it was the Spirit of the Moon. She called out to him and he stopped his sled and helped

her to get into it, covering her with many warm seal skins.

"Close your eyes," the Moon Spirit told the woman, "and do not open them until I tell you to. And when we get to my house you must not ever look in the direction of my sister the Sun, for if you do it will arouse her interest and she will burn you!"

So the woman kept her eyes closed until they arrived at the Moon's house.

When she opened her eyes and looked about, the Moon Spirit said again, "Do not look in the direction of the Sun!"

But the woman could not resist taking just one little sidelong glance in that direction, and immediately all of the fur was burned off her coat, so she did not look that way again.

The Moon Spirit entertained the woman with songs and she was given every sort of food to eat. He also opened a hatch in the floor and, blowing through a big pipe, showed her how he made the snow that fell on the earth. In this way a number of months passed.

Then one day the woman looked down through the opening in the floor and she could see all of the world below. She could see into every house and she watched the people in her own village and grew homesick. So the Moon Spirit got out his sled and took her home.

Not long afterward the woman gave birth to a son, and she was very happy. The baby grew to be a fine healthy young man and a good hunter, and when he was grown up, the Moon Spirit came again to visit and took the son away to live with him in the heavens.

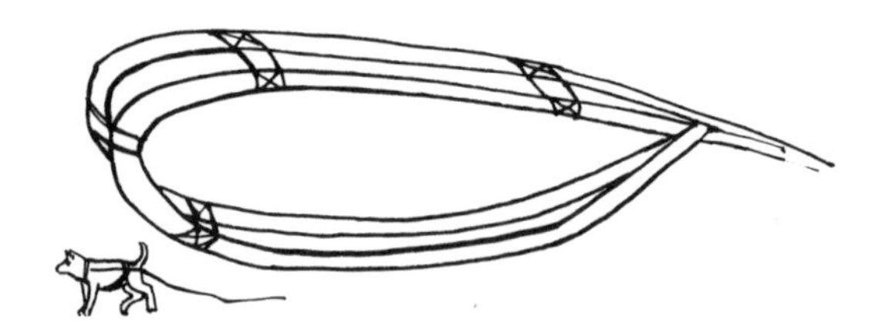

The First White Men

In ancient times, when igloos were alive and flew through the air with a rushing sound, and people burned snow in their lamps instead of oil (for in those days, snow did burn)—in those very ancient times, there was a man whose only daughter refused to marry.

First one and then another suitor came to her; fine men and good hunters asked her to marry them, but no one could please her.

Finally, the father grew so angry at his daughter that he said, "If no man can please you, then I will marry you to one of my dogs," and he did.

The couple went away to live on an island all by themselves, and the girl gave birth to ten children. Two of these children were Eskimos, two were dogs, and two were *erkileks*—dogs with men's heads; two were *qavdlunat*—white men, and two were *qavdlunatsait*—white men with warlike dispositions.

The girl put the four white men in the sole of a boot and set it adrift in the sea. (If you look at the hull of a ship from above, you will find that it looks exactly like the sole of a *kamik,* which is made of seal skin and is turned up all around.) The men drifted about until they came to the white men's land, and there they settled down and produced all of the white men that are now in the world.

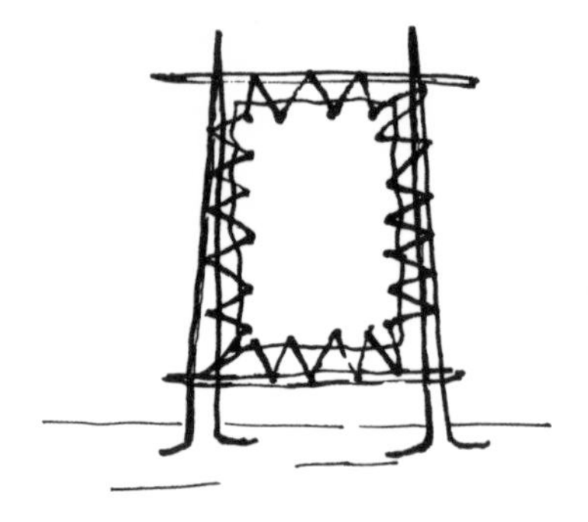

Sedna, the Sea Goddess

The Petrels, proud birds that they are, live on the highest parts of the cliffs. From their peaks they swirl out like snowflakes, looking down on the rolling noisiness of Razor Bills who build their nests halfway up, and the Gulls and the little Kittiwakes, who are content to nest at the bottom.

Once, long, long ago, there was a Petrel who was so proud that he could find no mate that pleased him among his own kind, so he decided that he would marry a human being.

With a little magic, the Petrel gave himself a human form. Then, wanting to look his best, he got some fine seal skins and made a beautiful parka. Now he looked very handsome, but his eyes were still the eyes of a bird, so he made some spectacles from thin pieces of walrus tusk. These spectacles had only narrow slits to look through, and hid the Petrel's eyes completely.

In this disguise, he went out in his kayak to find a wife.

In a skin-covered tent beside the sea there lived a beautiful girl named Sedna, who had many brothers but no sisters, and her father was a widower. Many men had come to her to ask her to marry them—men from her own tribe and other tribes—but Sedna refused to marry. She was as proud in her way as the Petrel, and could find no man who pleased her.

Then the Petrel came, appearing as a handsome stranger in a beautiful sealskin parka. Instead of bring-

ing his kayak up onto the beach, he stayed in it at the edge of the surf and called out to Sedna to come to him. This interested Sedna, as no other suitor had done such a thing, but she would not go to him.

Then he began to sing to her:

> "Come to me,
> Come into the land of the birds
> Where there is never hunger,
> Where my tent is made of beautiful skins.
> You will have a necklace of ivory
> And sleep on the skins of bears.
> Your lamps will be always filled with oil
> And your pot with meat."

The song was so beautiful that Sedna could not refuse. She packed her belongings in a sealskin bag; she stepped out of the tent and she walked down across the beach and got into the stranger's kayak. They sailed out over the sea, away from Sedna's home and her father and brothers.

The Petrel made a home for Sedna on the rocky cliff. Every day he caught fish for her, telling her that they were young seals, and for a while Sedna was happy, because the Petrel had enchanted her. But one day the Petrel's spectacles fell off, and for the first time Sedna looked into her husband's eyes. In that moment the spell was broken. She realized all at once that she was married to a bird, and she saw that her home was a nest on a barren cliff. For the first time she felt the sting of the sea spray and the lashing winds.

Sedna wept with grief and despair, and the Petrel, although he loved her, could not console her.

In the meantime, Sedna's father and brothers had grown more and more lonely, with no woman to cook their meat and sew their clothing and keep the oil burning in their lamps. They set out in their boat in the direction that the stranger had taken Sedna.

When they came to the cliff where Sedna lived, the Petrel was away hunting, and Sedna was alone. When she saw her family, she went running down to them, weeping, and in a rush told them all that had happened to her. Her brothers immediately lifted her into the boat and they began paddling as rapidly as possible back toward their own coast.

They had not been gone long when the Petrel returned to the nest. He looked everywhere for Sedna, and he called for her, his cry a long and lonely sound that was lost in the wind and the sound of the sea. Other Petrels answered him; they told him where Sedna had gone. Spreading his wings, he soared out over the sea and was soon flying over the boat that was carrying Sedna back to her home. This made the brothers nervous, and they paddled faster. As they skimmed over the water, the Petrel became angry. He began to beat his wings against the wind, making it whirl and shriek, and making the waves leap higher and higher. In minutes the sea was black with storm, and the waves so wild that the boat was in danger of turning over. Then Sedna's brothers and father realized that the Petrel was such a powerful spirit that even the sea was angry because his bride was being taken from him. They decided that they must sacrifice Sedna to the sea in order to save their own lives. They picked her up and threw her into the icy water.

Sedna, blue with cold, came up to the surface and grabbed at the side of the boat with fingers that were

turning to ice. Her brothers, out of their minds with fear, hit at her hands with a paddle, and her fingertips broke off like icicles and fell back into the sea, where they turned into seals and swam away. Coming up again, Sedna tried once more to catch hold of the boat, and again her brothers hit at her hands with the paddle. The second joints of her fingers, breaking off and falling into the water, turned into *ojuk,* ground seals. Two more times Sedna attempted to take hold of the side of the boat, and each time her terrified brothers hit her hands, and the third joints of her fingers turned into walrus and the thumbs became whales. Then Sedna sank to the bottom of the sea. The storm died down, and the brothers finally brought their boat to land, but a great wave followed them and drowned all of them.

Sedna became a powerful spirit, in control of the sea creatures who sprang from her fingers. Sometimes she sends storms and wrecks kayaks. The people fear her, and hold ceremonies in her honor, and on especially serious occasions—as when she causes famines by keeping the seals from being caught by the hunters—the *angakok*, or conjurer, goes on a spirit journey to Sedna's home at the bottom of the sea, to arrange her hair.

Sedna wears her hair in two braids, each as thick as an arm, but since she has no fingers, she cannot plait her own hair, and this is the service she appreciates most of all. So when the *angakok* comes to her and arranges her hair for her, she is so grateful that she sends some of the seals and other animals to the hunters so that they may have food.

Why the Raven Is Black

THE RAVEN and the Loon once agreed to tattoo each other. They put stones in a circle and inside the circle they built a fire, letting it burn down to charcoal. Then they pounded the charcoal down to a powder and put it in a stone box.

The Loon stood patiently for some time while the Raven decorated him, laboriously making markings on his wings with the end of a piece of bone dipped in the charcoal.

When the Raven had finished, the Loon began to tattoo him in his turn. The Raven, however, was difficult. He complained about the Loon's designs, and he shifted from one foot to the other and twisted his neck this way and that and fluttered his wings.

At last the Loon lost all patience. He picked up the box of charcoal and dumped it out over the Raven and ran away. As he was leaving, however, the Raven, who was very angry, picked up the fire stones and threw them at the Loon, injuring his legs so that the Loon could hardly walk.

Ever since that day, Ravens have been black all over, and Loons, when they are walking, have always looked as though they were about to fall down.

How the Guillemots Came

An old man once went out on the ice to look for breathing holes—the small holes, mounded over with snow, that tell us where the seals are. When the sea begins to freeze over, the seals make a number of breathing holes in the ice over their feeding grounds, so that if one freezes over there will be another to use. They make the rounds of these holes, taking a breath at each one, and keeping them open by scratching away any ice that has formed in the hole.

The old man finally found one of these breathing holes, and he prepared to wait for the seal to come to it. With his snow knife he cut a block of hard snow and put it down beside the breathing hole. He sat on it, facing the wind so that the seal would not catch his scent. He sat with his feet in a warm deerskin bag, his hands up his sleeves, and his spear across his knees. He knew that he might have a long wait until the seal came, but he was patient; he had nothing else to do.

Since he was an old man, he had not walked any great distance from the village, and not far from him, children were playing. They had chosen to play in a ravine that was sheltered from the wind by two steep walls of rock. As their voices, reverberating against the rocks, became louder and louder, the old man frowned and shouted at them, "Be quiet! You will frighten the seal away!"

The children were quieter for a little while, but gradually they forgot the old man and their voices began to rise higher and higher.

The old man, concentrating on the breathing hole, was suddenly aware of the soft sound of the seal scratching at the ice. He held his breath, and very quietly, his fur-parka sleeves making no sound, he grasped his spear and poised it ready. There was another sound from the breathing hole—a rough sigh as the seal exhaled the bad air it had been holding in its lungs as it swam under the ice. The old man made no move, knowing that the seal, after exhaling, would withdraw its head and listen for danger before putting its nose up for a deep breath of fresh air. It was for that moment

that the old man was waiting—the moment when the seal thrust its nose up through the breathing hole and inhaled deeply. It was then and only then that the hunter must drive his spear home, deep into the seal's neck.

But at that very moment there was a great burst of laughter from the ravine where the children were playing, and the seal, hearing it, dived quickly down into the sea beneath the ice. The old man had missed his chance.

"See what you have done!" he shouted at the children, "You have frightened away my catch!"

The children were silent for some time after that, and the old man sat humped over the breathing hole, waiting resignedly for the seal's next appearance. By the time the seal came again to the hole, however, the children had forgotten, and once more their noise frightened the seal away.

The old man was beside himself with anger and frustration and he screamed, "Oh, rocks, close over them!"

At his words, which were magic words, the cleft in the rocks closed over the children, imprisoning them in the ravine. They could only look up through small openings in the top of the ravine and cry for help.

One girl, who was older than the others, and was taking care of a baby for a woman in the village, began to sing, trying to comfort the child:

"Do not weep, little one.
Your mother will fetch you.
Mother is coming for you
As soon as she has finished her new *kamiks*.
Do not weep, little one.
Your father will fetch you.
Father is coming for you
As soon as he has made his new harpoon head.
Do not weep, little one,
Do not weep."

But the children continued to weep. Their cries soon brought the people from the village. They came run-

ning, to find their children hopelessly trapped in the cleft of the rocks. There was nothing that anyone could do to get the children out.

The old man still sat at the seal hole, waiting for his seal, and the people, seeing him, and finding that it was he who was responsible for the cleft closing, became very angry and shouted at him, "May you be changed to frost!"

Just then the children, still crying, came flying out of the cleft, for they had all turned into guillemots, the black-and-white gull-like birds that, from that day to this, have nested in the fissures of rocks by the sea.

When the old man did not come home for supper, his wife went hunting for him and found him still sitting on his block of snow beside the seal hole. She began scraping away at the frost and rime that covered him, thinking that it was a thin layer the wind had blown over him. She scraped and scraped, and at last there was nothing left of the old man at all, because he had become nothing but frost.

The First Narwhal

A LONG TIME AGO a widow lived with her two children, a daughter named Nayagta, and a son, Tutigak. The son, when he became a young man, was a good hunter, and one day he caught a large thong-seal. When he brought it home, his mother said, "That skin will make a fine sleeping-ledge cover."

But Tutigak said no, he wanted to make it into hunting lines for his harpoon.

The mother became angry about this, and as she prepared the skin, scraping it and softening it, she said magic words over it:

> "When he cuts thee into thongs,
> When he cuts thee asunder,
> Then thou shalt snap and strike his face!"

And she smiled to herself, thinking of the leather hitting him. She finished preparing the skin and gave it to Tutigak, and as he cut the first thong from it, stretching it out, it snapped back and hit his eyes, and in that moment he became blind.

Now, Tutigak could no longer hunt. He sat on the ledge throughout most of the winter, while his mother and sister gathered mussels, which were their only food.

In the middle of the winter, however, a large bear came to the igloo, and began to eat away the window, which was made of strips of transparent animal membranes sewn together. The mother and sister were frightened, and cowered at the farthest corner of the sleeping ledge, but Tutigak told his sister to bring his

bow. She brought it to him and he bent it. Nayagta aimed it for him and gave him a signal and Tutigak shot. The arrow killed the bear instantly and it fell to the ground just outside the window.

The mother lied, "That was the window you struck, instead of the bear." But Nayagta whispered to her brother, "You have killed the bear!"

Now they had meat for many days, but the mother continued to feed Tutigak mussels, never giving him any of the bear meat. His sister gave him bear meat, however, whenever the mother went out, and Tutigak had to eat it hurriedly before she came back.

At last the long winter was over, and the days were getting longer. Nayagta said to her brother, "Do you remember how beautiful everything was last year, when you could see, and could go hunting, and we went out into the hills?"

"Oh, yes," said Tutigak. "Take hold of my hand and lead me up to the lake."

The brother and sister walked through the fields to the edge of the lake. The scent of the spring flowers came strongly to Tutigak, reminding him of other times when he had been able to see, when he had been a whole man and a hunter.

As Nayagta and Tutigak stood beside the lake a loon flew down and alighted beside them.

"Take hold of my neck," the loon said to Tutigak, "and I will carry you."

Tutigak put his arms around the bird's neck, and it dived down into the lake with him. When it seemed that the young man could hold his breath no longer, they came to the surface, but immediately went down into the depths again, then up and down once more before the loon brought Tutigak once again out into the air. Tutigak was gasping and sputtering.

"Can you see the land?" asked the loon.

Tutigak shook the water from his eyes and opened them wide. Then he shouted joyfully, "I see!"

The loon immediately dived down again with him into the water and when he came back up, asked:

"What do you see now?"

"I see wide countries!" exclaimed Tutigak.

The loon took Tutigak back to his sister and then flew away. The brother and sister walked home through the spring meadows, full of joy.

When they came into their home, Tutigak remarked, "What a fine bear skin!"

His mother realized that he could see again, but all that she said was, "It is a skin that a friend has left us." This was a lie, because the skin was really that of the bear that Tutigak had killed with his bow and arrow.

Now that he had his sight back, Tutigak began to hunt and fish again. It was the season when the white whales appeared off the coast, and Tutigak, with Na-

yagta's help, would catch them. The two would go out on the ice along the shore, and Tutigak would tie his long hunting line around Nayagta's waist. Then he would aim and throw the harpoon that was attached to the other end of the line and when he had speared the whale, the brother and sister would pull together on the line until they had brought it up on the beach. Tutigak called Nayagta his "hunting bladder" because a hunter usually attached the inflated bladder of a seal to his hunting line. The bladder would bring up the catch, or the harpoon, if the weapon missed its mark, by floating to the surface. Tutigak was careful to strike only the smallest of the white whales, so that Nayagta would not be pulled into the water.

The mother, watching the white whales off shore, and being greedy, complained that Tutigak should catch the larger ones. So the next day Tutigak asked her to be his hunting bladder in place of Nayagta. Then when he had tied the hunting line to the old woman's waist, he threw his harpoon out, hitting the largest of the white whales. As the whale dived down into the sea, the line grew taut and whipped out of Tutigak's hands. The old woman was jerked off her feet and pulled down the beach into the water.

"My knife! My knife!" she screamed, for she had nothing with which to cut the line, but before anyone

could help her, she had disappeared into the sea, and she was never seen again.

The white whales also disappeared, and Tutigak and Nayagta, feeling sad and guilty, went back to their home. They no longer wanted to live where they had lived with their wicked mother, and they determined to go far away to the interior of the country. There they lived quite alone and apart from all other people until they grew very old and their hair turned white.

The wicked mother, deep in the ocean, changed into a narwhal—a great horned whale—her heavy, plaited hair becoming a long, spiraling horn. It is said that from her, all narwhals are descended.

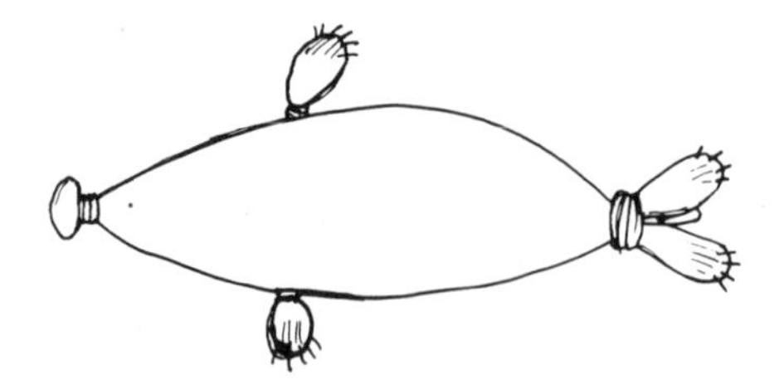

Kasiagsak Who Lied

OF ALL THE MEN in the village, Kasiagsak was the poorest hunter. While others brought home seals and walrus to their wives for food and skins, Kasiagsak never did.

For one thing, he always felt a little sorry for the seals. One day he saw a black spot out in the sea on a piece of ice, and he paddled slowly toward it, hoping that it would not be a seal, but it was.

"Poor little thing," Kasiagsak said to himself. "It seems a pity to harpoon it."

He sat in his kayak for a time, watching the seal, and it occurred to him that perhaps someone had already wounded it.

"If it is wounded, then all I need to do is go up to it and take hold of it with my hands."

So he started toward it, making quite a lot of noise, and of course the seal slipped into the sea and was gone in no time.

"Ah, well," said Kasiagsak, "maybe next time!"

Kasiagsak's wife was having a hard time, with no meat and no skins, and it embarrassed her that she must always accept these things from others in the village and never be able to return the favors. For this reason she was cross with Kasiagsak and scolded him every time he returned home empty handed from a day's hunting.

Kasiagsak decided that he must bring home a seal somehow, and one day as he was out in his kayak he noticed that some of the other men had harpooned a

large seal, and had drawn it up on the beach and secured it with a towing line to a rock while they went on to find some more.

Kasiagsak pretended to pay no attention, but as soon as the other hunters were out of sight he paddled in to the beach where the seal had been left and carried it home with him. He was especially pleased with the towing line with which the seal was tied, as it was decorated in an unusual manner with walrus teeth.

His wife saw him coming home and was delighted to see that he was pulling a large seal behind him. "Well!" she said to her neighbors. "Now it is *my* turn to share my husband's catch with *you!*"

As she began to strip the seal, she noticed the towing line and she asked, "Where did you get this beautiful towing line?"

Kasiagsak told her that he'd had it for a long time.

"Really?" asked his wife, but she was so busy cutting up the seal that she thought no more about it.

Later that evening a boy came to Kasiagsak and said, "I have been sent for the towing line. As for the seal, that doesn't matter."

Kasiagsak gave him the towing line and the boy went away.

"Kasiagsak!" cried his wife. "Did you lie to me?"

"As a matter of fact, I did," said Kasiagsak, and at

this his wife began to scold him, but he only lay down on the sleeping ledge and began to whistle. He whistled far into the night so that his wife could not sleep.

The next time Kasiagsak went hunting, he saw a black spot out on the ice and he paddled slowly toward it, hoping that it was a rock, and it was. So he tied his hunting bladder to the rock and rolled it into the sea with a great splash. Then he paddled back to the others and told them that he had harpooned a walrus, but unfortunately it had dived to the bottom of the sea with his hunting bladder.

"We will help you to catch it!" said the others, but Kasiagsak hurried off, saying that he would go home and tell his wife what had happened.

His wife was very happy to hear that he had harpooned a walrus. "Now," she cried, "I can have a new handle to my knife and a new hook for my kettle!"

Soon the other men came back, carrying Kasiagsak's hunting bladder, and they said, "We found it tied to a stone."

Then Kasiagsak's wife was angry and she scolded him again.

Kasiagsak thought that if only he could have a terrible accident of some sort, his wife would feel sorry for him and perhaps the people would think him a hero.

So the next day he went to a deserted beach where there were many pieces of loose ice, and he filled his kayak with ice and stuffed pieces of ice down into his clothing, and walked out into the water up to his neck, so that his clothing was soaked through. He did not know that two women were picking berries not far away from him, and saw everything that he did.

Kasiagsak hurried home to his wife and cried out to her, "An iceberg has burst and fallen right across my kayak! It is a wonder I escaped alive!"

His wife was very worried about him, and as soon as she had given him dry clothing, she went out and told all of the women in the village about the terrible accident that had happened to her husband.

Just then the two women who had been picking berries returned and they said to Kasiagsak's wife, "We saw your husband down on the beach, stuffing his clothing with ice! Why was he doing that?"

Now Kasiagsak's wife was really angry, and she scolded him so much that he could not even whistle.

The next day when Kasiagsak was out in his kayak he saw a piece of whale skin floating on the water and he paddled back to the other hunters and cried out to them, "I have found a whale!"

The others asked, "Where? Where? Take us to it!"

Kasiagsak began paddling out to sea, the others following him. They went farther and farther, and the others kept asking, "Where is it?"

Kasiagsak would say, "Just a little farther."

At last the others gave up and turned back, but Kasiagsak kept on paddling out to sea, and he was never seen again.

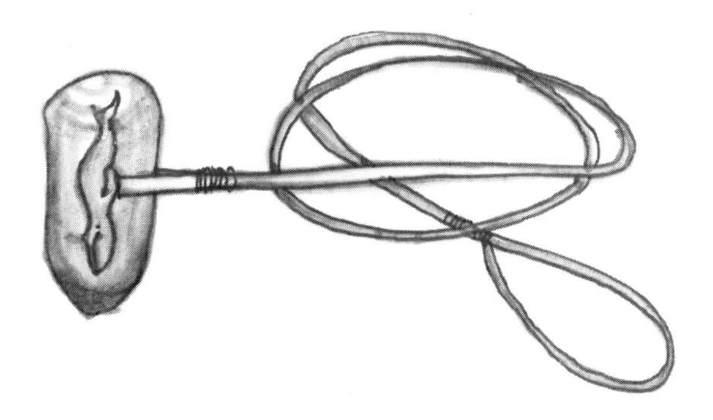

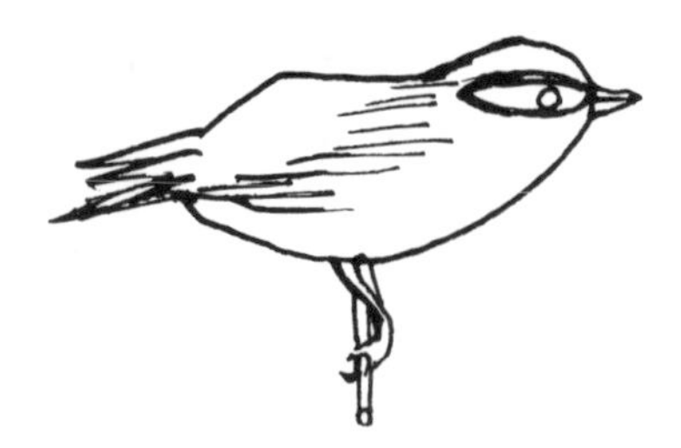

How the Sea Ravens Came To Be

THERE WAS ONCE a raven who wanted more than anything to get married. He went first to see a little sparrow who had recently lost her husband. She had been very fond of her husband, who brought her many worms.

As the sparrow sat in the grass, grieving and weeping, the raven came to her and said, "You should not be weeping and grieving. You can marry me! Just look at my wonderfully high forehead, and my broad temples and my long beard and my big beak! Marry me!"

The sparrow looked at him. "No," she said. "I will not marry you, and the reason I will not marry you is that you have a very high forehead and broad temples and a long beard and a big beak."

The raven flew away, so lovesick that he had trouble sleeping. He came to some geese who were getting ready to fly south for the winter. The raven picked out two of the geese and asked them to marry him.

"We were just leaving," said the geese.

The raven said he would go along.

"You can't," said the geese. "You will not be able to fly so far without stopping, and you are not able to rest by floating on the water, the way we can."

"Never mind that," said the raven, and he married the two geese.

They immediately began their flight out over the open sea, and they had not gone far before the raven was too tired to go farther.

"I must have something to rest on!" he cried, and he told his wives to alight on the water close beside each other so that he could rest on their backs. Comfortable, and so tired, the raven went to sleep.

Soon the raven's wives looked up and saw that the other geese were almost out of sight on the distant horizon. With a great flapping of their wings, the two shook off their husband and flew off to catch up with the others.

The raven, with a loud cry, fell into the sea and sank to the bottom, where he broke into many tiny pieces. These pieces became the sea ravens, those little black creatures that swim about the sea, their flippers looking so much like wings.

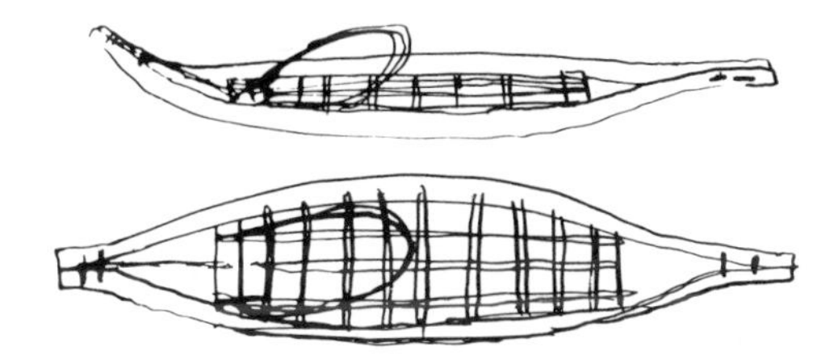

The Angakok

In the winter, in the long darkness and the deep cold, men sometimes think of the hidden things—of the mysteries of death and what comes after. (For something must come after; it would be unreasonable if after this life, one ceased to exist.) When *Oqaloraq*, the spirit who lives in the hollow places of the snowdrift where the wind whines and blows the most, is laughing in the storm and the hill spirits are about, then men think most often of the hidden things that are not to be understood.

Most of the time, of course, ordinary men do not think very much about such things, being too busy with hunting and eating.

There are, however, men who are not ordinary.

There are men who are more simple than most, or less simple, men to whom spirits show themselves and to whom secrets are revealed. Such a man was Ataitsiak.

Even when he was quite young, Ataitsiak knew that he wanted to be an *angakok*, a conjurer. Therefore he went up into the hills, far away, and up into the rocks, away from people, and prepared to spend the night there, for the power of solitude is great and beyond understanding.

There appeared before him two hill spirits. Ataitsiak said nothing to them; the spirits sang some drum songs. The next day Ataitsiak went home, but he said nothing of his experience because he was humble, and knew that he was only just beginning to be an *angakok*. Not

long after this, he went hunting and being tired he lay down beside a large rock. There the hill spirits appeared to him again, singing drum songs. The third time the spirits appeared to Ataitsiak in his own home, and then he knew that they were his *tornaks*—helpful spirits, and that he would really be an *angakok*. For an *angakok* does not choose his *tornaks*; they choose him, and come of their own accord.

Ataitsiak then went to the most powerful *angakok* in his village and said to him, "*Takujumangama,*" which means, "I come to you because I desire to see." From that day on, Ataitsiak was apprenticed to the *angakok*, learning from him the many things that a conjurer must know: He must learn the special spirit language, in which one converses with and about spirits. He must be able to see himself as a skeleton, freed from everything that is perishable. He must learn the sacred rites and ceremonies, the lore of the people, and all of the ancient songs. He must confess any wrongs that he has done, must fast and abstain from many things, must wear his hair long, eat with his hands covered, and go to bed without getting undressed. Most important of all, he must be able to go into a trance; his soul must be able to go on journeys away from his body, to the moon and to the bottom of the sea.

When Ataitsiak had experienced enlightenment, a

sudden light within his body and within his head, and he could see into the future and understand secrets, then he was a true *angakok*, with the power to detect guilt and heal the sick.

Ataitsiak had a hunting place not far from his home where he always hunted alone. One day he harpooned a seal and as he was about to pull it in, the seal gave a sudden sharp pull and capsized Ataitsiak's kayak. Ataitsiak was thrown into the icy water. He was so startled that it was a minute or two before he thought to call his *tornaks*, but as soon as he did, they appeared, coming across the sea in kayaks. One righted his kayak and drained the water from it, and the other replaced Ataitsiak in it, and gave him warm, dry clothes.

As he began to thaw out and get his bearings, Ataitsiak noticed that the three kayaks were now headed out to sea. They soon came to a strange land, and they drew the kayaks up on the beach before a village, where people came out to meet them. That evening Ataitsiak stayed in one of the family igloos in the village, and was fed many kinds of food. After he had eaten all that he could, he lay back to rest, and it was then that he noticed, at the back of the sleeping ledge, a young man who looked very ill.

An old man said to Ataitsiak, "This is a very sad case. This young man used to be a very great hunter, and he kept us all in meat, even in the worst weather. Now we know that something strange ails him. Will you examine him?"

Ataitsiak of course said that he would, but as he prepared to do so, he noticed an evil spirit coming close to the young man. The others could not see the spirit.

Now Ataitsiak began his conjurations and it was revealed to him that the evil spirit was that of the young man's old aunt, who lived nearby, and was a witch. The following evening as they all gathered around the sick young man, Ataitsiak again saw the evil spirit, and he said, "I must tell you the truth; it is the evil spirit of the old woman who is doing this young man harm. If he is to get well I must kill her."

Then he took his harpoon, and asked the men to help him by holding onto the lines of it, as the evil spirit was very powerful. As long as the spirit looked at Ataitsiak, he was unable to throw his harpoon at her, but finally she glanced away, and Ataitsiak threw the harpoon, but so quick was the spirit that she was already diving down through a hole that suddenly appeared in the floor, and the spear caught her only in the foot. She disappeared through the hole, dragging the harpoon with her, and all of the men holding the line could not stop it, although Ataitsiak finally managed to hold it fast.

"Now," he told the others, "Go and see how the old aunt is."

They went and found that she was on her sleeping ledge, with a bleeding foot.

The next day Ataitsiak went home, and several weeks later many kayaks appeared, coming to visit his village, bringing gifts. Among the people in the kayaks was the young man, quite healthy again, and he told Ataitsiak that his old aunt, the witch, had died.

This was only one of many deeds that Ataitsiak did, as he was a very great *angakok*.

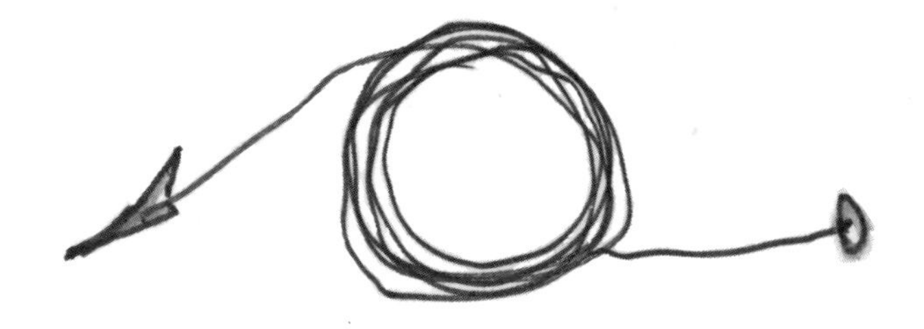

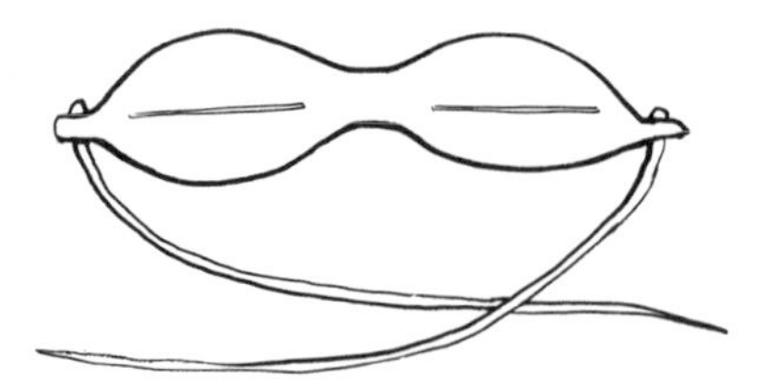

How the Light Came

At one time the whole world was in darkness, because the Chief of the Sky kept the ball of light in a box in his house, and would only let out a tiny bit of light for the people to use.

The Raven, being very wise, and also supernatural, knew all this, and he felt sorry for the people. They would grope around in the dark, trying to catch *oolichans,* but because they could not see what they were doing, the little fish kept slipping away from them.

Finally the Raven decided to get the ball of light away from the Chief of the Sky. He started out, and he flew for a long time, until he came to a place where a river ran between two very high, steep banks, quite close together. At the end of this gorge there was a very bright light. The Raven sat in a tree to rest and as he sat there he noticed that the gorge was opening and closing. He waited until it opened up and then he flew through it as fast as he could. The gorge closed up just as he got through it.

Now he was in the land of the Chief of the Sky, and the light was almost blinding. The Raven flew on until he came to a beautiful lake with a great house beside it, and he knew this was the Sky Chief's home, so he sat down on a branch of a spruce tree that grew beside the lake. He noticed that everyone came to this spot to get water, and he waited until the Chief's daughter came. As she dipped up some water, the raven quickly changed himself into a spruce needle, dropped into the

lake, and the girl swallowed him as she drank. Some months later, the Chief's daughter gave birth to a baby boy, and this was the Raven.

Now the baby boy became the main delight of the Chief of the Sky, and the old man kept the baby close to him at all times, not even letting anyone else feed him. He gave the baby anything he wanted.

After a while, the baby began to cry all the time. He cried, "Ball! Ball!" and this worried the old Chief. He tried everything he could think of, but nothing would make the baby stop crying. Finally he called in his wise men and asked them what was the matter with his grandson. The wise men tried one thing and then another thing, and finally one said, "Maybe he wants the ball of light that you keep in the box."

The Chief immediately got down the ball of light and gave it to the baby, and the baby stopped crying and began playing very happily with the ball. After a short time, the baby appeared to lose interest in the ball, and the Chief put it away.

After this, the baby played often with the ball, and gradually everyone got used to it and no one paid any attention. This was what the Raven had been waiting for. One day when the Chief and his servants were in another part of the house, the baby rolled the ball out the door, crawling after it, and as soon as he was out-

side he changed himself back into a raven and flew away with the ball of light.

He flew back through the gorge, and came at last to the people who were still trying to catch *oolichans* in the dark. The Raven alighted on the beach and at once he burst the ball of light, so that the whole world was full of brightness, and the people could see to catch the *oolichans*.

The people heard the caw of the Raven when the light burst upon them, and so they knew who had done it, and they shared their *oolichans* with him, and have done so ever since.

How the Fog Came

THERE WAS ONCE a bear who went down into the villages to steal meat from the meat caches. Every night more meat disappeared, and finally one of the men of the village decided to catch whoever was stealing the meat. He went to the meat cache in the evening and lay down to wait until the thief came. He waited and waited and at last he fell asleep. It was then that the bear came, and seeing the man and thinking him dead, it picked him up, threw him over one shoulder, and started back to its home.

The man awoke as the bear was throwing him over its shoulder, but realizing what had happened, he decided that his best chance was to play dead. Therefore, he made himself as heavy as possible, and every time the bear went past a willow tree, the man would hold onto the branches and the bear would be caught off balance.

By the time it had arrived at its home, the bear was very tired indeed. It dropped the man on the floor and lay down to sleep. The bear's wife went out to gather wood for a fire.

The bear's children were dancing around the man, very happy at the thought of the dinner he would make, when the man opened his eyes and looked around.

"Look! Look, father!" the bear's children shouted. "He is opening his eyes!"

The bear awoke but only growled, "Nonsense!" and went back to sleep.

Then the man jumped up and quickly killed the bear and its children, and ran out of the house.

The bear's wife, seeing the running figure and thinking it her husband, cried, "Where are you going?"

The man did not answer, but ran on faster than ever. The bear's wife, becoming suspicious, ran after him.

The man looked back and saw that she was gaining on him and so he spoke some magic words:

"Rise up!
 Rise up, mountains!"

A ridge of mountains immediately rose up between the man and the bear's wife. It took her quite a while to scramble up over the mountains, and the man got ahead, but soon she was gaining on him again. He saw a little stream and leaped across it and then spoke some more magic words:

"Overflow!
 Overflow, stream!"

At these words the little stream spread out and deepened until it was impossible to cross. The bear's wife stopped at the edge and called across to the man, "How did you get across this stream?"

The man called back, "I drank the water. Drink it dry!"

The bear's wife began to drink the water. She drank and drank until she was swollen several times her size with the water.

Then the man shouted suddenly, "Look at your tail!"

The bear's wife, wondering what was the matter with her tail, quickly bent over to peer between her legs, but she was so full of water that this caused her to burst. As she did so, the water came from her in many tiny drops like steam, and this became fog, which has ever since that day drifted about between the mountains.

Avunang

THERE WAS ONCE a man named Avunang, who could not be killed. One time he went with his wife to a village in the south, to trade for wood, which could not be found in his own village. While on the way, enemies came along and attacked Avunang and threw him down through a seal hole in the ice, into the sea. Thinking him dead, his wife sorrowfully started back toward her home. Avunang's enemies went on toward the south. Eventually they saw a seal ahead of them, and they drove after it, racing across the thin ice, until the ice gave way and half of the party fell through into the sea and were drowned.

The others went on for a time and they saw a fox ahead of them in the snow. They started after it and the fox went faster and faster, and led them up over a ridge that was too steep for the sleds. They fell down the other side, killing all of the remaining men except two, who managed to reach the village and told of what had happened.

Now, it was Avunang's soul that had changed to a seal, and then to a fox, in order to kill his enemies. This was such an interesting experience that Avunang decided that he would try living in all of the animals that were in the world, so that he could tell people what it was like.

For a while he was a dog, but he did not like being a dog, because men were always beating him.

Then he was a reindeer.

"What do you eat?" he asked the other reindeer, and they told him, "Moss and lichen," so he ate that, not liking it very much.

"How do you run so fast?" he asked them and they said, "Kick toward the outside edge of heaven." So he did, but he still had trouble keeping up.

On a day when wolves attacked the reindeer, Avunang decided it would be better to be a wolf, but he found that it was the same as it had been with the reindeer. He could not keep up.

"Kick up toward heaven," they told him, just as the reindeer had, and so he did, but he did not like being always on the run as the wolves were.

So he became a walrus, but he could not dive very well.

"Kick your back feet up toward heaven!" they told him, and he did and then he could dive, but he did not like always eating mussels and shellfish.

For a while he was a raven, but his feet were always cold.

He was even a louse, once.

He lived in every animal that was in the world, and then he became a man again and went home to his wife.

Forever after, when the people gathered in the singing house to sing and tell their stories, there was no one who could tell tales as wonderful as those of Avunang, who knew the thoughts of all animals, and could make in his throat the growling of bears, the howling of wolves, and the calls of all the birds.

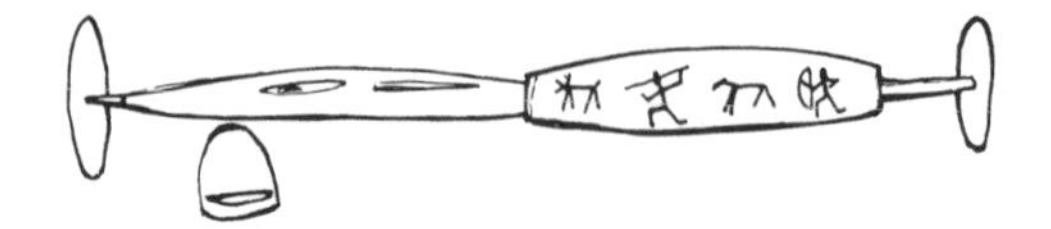

The Girls Who Chose Strange Husbands

THERE WERE ONCE four young girls playing on the beach, and they pretended to choose husbands. One girl saw a whale spouting out at sea, and she said, "I will take a whale for a husband!"

The second girl saw an eagle flying overhead and she said, "I will marry an eagle!"

The third girl saw a sea scorpion in the shallow water, and she said, "I will be the sea scorpion's wife!"

The fourth girl looked around for something to marry, and just then some men came along in kayaks and asked her to marry them. The girl was very hard to please, and none of the men pleased her. Just then she happened to look at a stone on the beach, and she said, "I would rather marry a stone!"

Now, the whale, the eagle, the sea scorpion, and the stone heard all of this.

At that moment, the fourth girl began to turn into a stone. She felt it first in her feet, and she became frightened and called out to the men in the kayak, "Come back! I have changed my mind!"

The kayakers had begun to paddle away.

Now the girl's legs were turning to stone, and she called to the men for help, but they had been offended, and would not listen.

The girl went on turning to stone, little by little, and when her heart had turned to stone, then she was indeed married to the stone.

While this was going on, the sea scorpion came and

carried off the third girl to his hole among the rocks and she was never found again.

Then an eagle swooped down and carried off the second girl. The girl's family followed, in their boat, to the steep cliff where the eagle had its nest. The girl had made ropes from sinews and let herself down to the boat, while the eagle was away, and so she got safely back to her home.

Now a whale carried off the first girl, and took her to an island, where he made a house for her from his own bones. He was so fond of the girl that he would not let her out of his sight for a minute, but the girl kept watching for a chance to escape.

One day her family, who had come in their boat to

rescue her, arrived at the island, and the girl, who was always watching, saw them before the whale did, and managed to slip out and get into the boat. They paddled away as fast as they could.

The whale saw at once that the girl was gone, but he had to take the house apart and put his bones back in his body, so it was a little while before he caught up with the boat.

When the girl's family saw the whale close behind them, they threw out one of the girl's *kamiks,* and the whale stopped, thinking it was the girl. By the time he had found that it was only her *kamik,* the boat was ahead again. They kept doing this, throwing out first the other *kamik,* and then the girl's parka, and then her trousers, and the whale stopped for each piece of clothing. In this way they came to their own shore, ahead of the whale. The whale was close behind, and leaped onto the beach after the boat. But he died on the beach because in his hurry to put his bones back in, he had forgotten his hip bones and could not get back into the water.

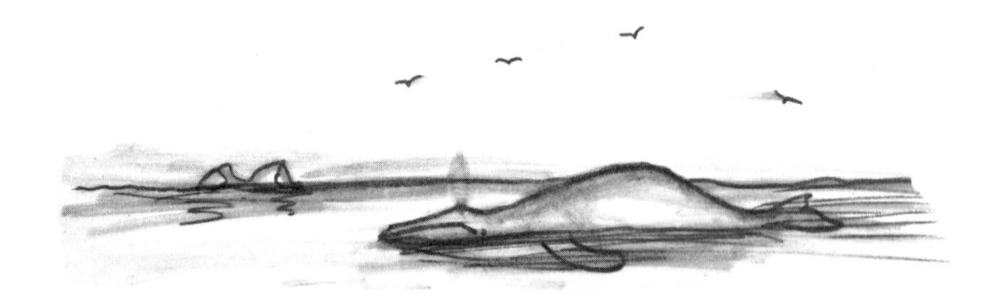

Qalutaligssuaq

THERE IS A terrible monster who lives in the sea and his name is Qalutaligssuaq, which means "he with the ladles." The reason for his name is that this monster makes a noise that sounds like two wooden ladles being banged together. People often hear this sound from the sea.

More than anything else, Qalutaligssuaq likes to eat children who make too much noise.

One day some children were playing on the beach, screaming and shouting and making a great deal of noise, and the monster came up out of the sea, clicking and clacking, the water streaming from his sides, and his mouth open wide.

The children ran for the hills as fast as they could,

across the rocky beach, but there was one child, an orphan, who could not keep up. He had no shoes, and the rocks hurt his feet.

The monster came closer and closer, and the orphan saw that he would not be able to escape. When he could feel Qalutaligssuaq's breath on the back of his neck, the orphan threw himself down on the ground and stuck his foot into the monster's face. He waggled his big toe back and forth right under the monster's nose, and said, "Watch out for my big toe; it eats men!"

At this, Qalutaligssuaq was so terrified that he turned around and splashed back into the sea.

The Man and the Star

ONE EVENING a man and his son went down to the beach and they sat there for a while, looking at the stars. There were a great many stars, but one in particular seemed to the boy to be off by itself. It looked lonely. He said to it, "Poor little fellow! You must be cold, up there!"

The star heard this, and the next evening when the boy was out of the house, alone, the star came down and took him up to the sky. This sometimes happens to people who talk to stars.

In the morning, the people of the village looked everywhere, but the boy could not be found. They asked people from other villages, but no one had seen him. Finally all of the people gave up looking, except

the boy's parents. They cried all the time; they missed him so much.

One day the father went out walking, still looking for his son, and he saw a mountain smoking. He climbed the mountain and near the top, where the smoke was coming out, he met an old woman.

The old woman said to the man, "Do you know who stole your child?"

The man said no, he did not know, and the woman told him that the star had stolen the boy.

"The star keeps your son tied up, and the boy cries all the time, because he is homesick," said the old woman. "If you want to get him back, you must go and make many arrows."

The man went back home and made four bundles of arrows, and then he climbed back up the mountain to the very top, and he took his bow and shot an arrow at the sky. The arrow hit near a hole in the sky, and there it stuck. Then the man shot another arrow, hitting the feathered end of the first arrow, and then he shot another in the same way, and he went on doing this for a number of days. At last the arrows reached down to the top of the mountain and the man could climb up to the hole in the sky.

He made a bundle containing red paint and tobacco and sling stones, and he started out, climbing the arrows until he reached the sky.

There he met a person who said, "The star watches

your son closely, but if you put in his place a wooden figure carved to look like the boy, the star may not notice for a while that the boy is gone."

The man gave this person some of the tobacco and red paint and sling stones, to thank him for his advice, and the person was very happy.

Then the man carved a piece of wood to look like his son, and went on until he met another person.

This person told the man to wait until the star was asleep, and then to go very quietly around the house to the other side where the boy was tied.

The man thanked this person as he had the other, with tobacco and red paint and sling stones. This person tasted the tobacco and immediately swelled up very big. Tobacco did that to him.

The father waited till the star was asleep and then he crept very quietly around the house to where his son was tied. The boy was very happy to see his father and he stopped crying, and the father untied him and put the wooden figure in his place, and they started hurrying back in the way they had come.

The star awoke and noticed that the boy was not crying. He looked out and saw the wooden figure so he went back to sleep. In the early morning, however, the star went out and discovered that the boy was gone and realized that the father had come and taken him away.

He said to his people, "Run after them!" and they did so.

When the man looked around and saw the star and his people close behind him, he threw tobacco and red paint and sling stones in the path in front of them. The star's people stopped and some took the sling stones, which were blue, and some took the red paint and painted themselves with it. This gave the man and his son a chance to get ahead again. Soon, however, they heard the star's people close behind them again. They had come to the place where the person who had swollen up from the tobacco was standing. The man gave this person some more tobacco and the person grew so much that the star's people could not get past.

So the man and the boy came to the hole in the sky and climbed down the chain of arrows. As soon as they got to the mountain top the man pulled the arrows all down to the ground. Then they went down the mountain to their home and the mother was very happy to see them.

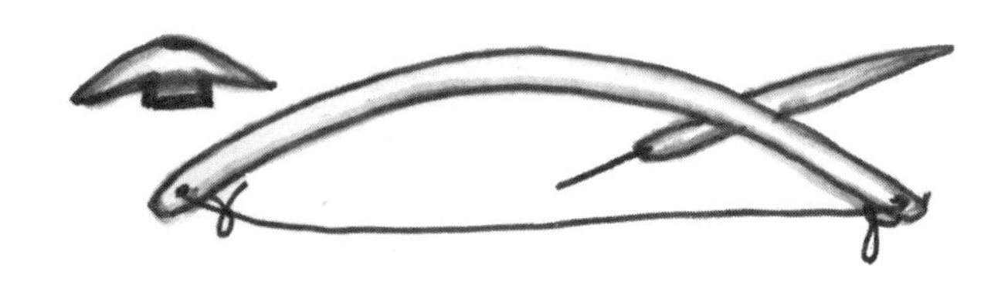

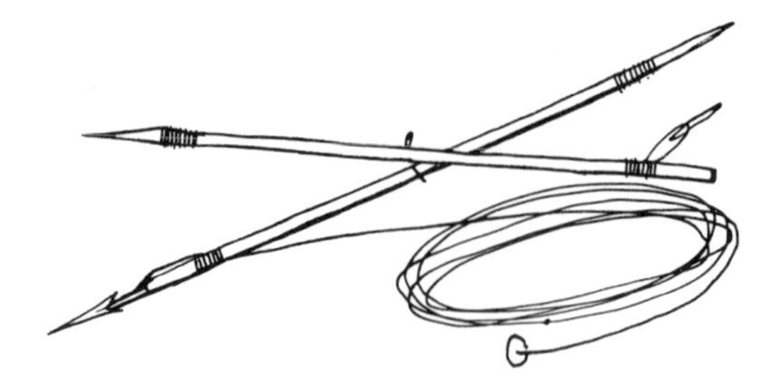

The Dragon

THERE WAS ONCE a chief's daughter who was not quite old enough to be a woman, nor young enough to be a little girl. Because she was neither child nor woman, but almost a woman, she had to leave her home and go to live all alone for a while, in a little hut at the edge of the village. This was the custom of her people. She was very lonely, for the only person she ever saw was the old woman who brought her food once a day. As the hours and the days went by she wished many times for someone to talk to, for someone to play with.

One day she saw a little white worm come crawling out from under the wall of the hut. She was so lonely that even a worm seemed very wonderful, and she picked it up and talked to it, and fed it some of her food. The next day the worm had grown much larger, and the girl was so delighted that she sang, "It has a mouth already! Sit right up, here! Sit right up!"

When she sang this little song, the worm opened its mouth very wide, for more food, and the girl fed it. The next day, the worm was even larger, and the girl sang, "It has a face already! Sit right up, here! Sit right up!"

The worm opened its mouth wide, and she fed it some more food. Each day, the worm grew larger and larger, and ate more and more food, until the girl no longer had enough to satisfy it, and so it began to crawl about the village, stealing the food of all the people. When the people found their oil boxes empty, they

began to hunt for the thief. Finally the girl's father, the chief, saw the monstrous worm, crawling along behind the little hut. As the chief watched, his daughter came to the door, clapped her hands and sang to the terrible creature, "Sit right up, here! Sit right up!"

At that, the monster opened its mouth wide—so wide that the chief could see far down its throat, and it was like a great cave. The chief cried out to his daughter, "What have you done! We must get rid of this. I will kill it at once!"

This made the girl cry, for she loved the dragon, having known it when it was only a little worm. When the girl cried, the dragon roared, and the chief ran away, frightened, to warn the rest of the village.

"We must all get out of here," he told the people. "We must take all our belongings that we can carry, and leave, or the dragon will surely kill us all!"

So the people gathered their belongings together, and formed a long procession and left the village, walking one behind another, single file. As they left the gates of the village, they walked into a large cave, where they thought to hide, but it was really the great, open mouth of the dragon, who was waiting for them. As soon as the dragon saw that all the people had walked into his mouth, he closed it, *snap*! and lay there smiling to himself.

The people had forgotten about the chief's daughter, who still sat alone in her little hut. When a day went by and no one had brought her food, she went down to the village to see what had happened. She went first to her father's house, and then to every house in the village, and there was no sign of any living being.

She felt very frightened and lonely. Finally she went out the gate of the village, and there lay her dragon, smiling to himself. In the silence of the place, the girl heard singing, as though it came from underground, or from very far away. It was her people, inside the dragon, singing to keep their courage.

When the chief's daughter realized that the dragon had swallowed the whole village, she sat down by the

gate and began to weep, wishing that she had not been so foolish, and that her father had killed the monster.

While she sat weeping, a young chief from a distant tribe came along and asked her why she was so sad. The girl told him all that had happened. When the young man understood that the mysterious singing came from the people inside the dragon, he said to the girl, "First, we must make the dragon open its mouth!"

Then the girl remembered the little song she had sung to the dragon when it was still a little worm, and she began to sing, "Sit right up, here! Sit right up!"

When the dragon heard this, he opened his mouth wide, and all the people came running out. Then the young chief killed the dragon with his spear, and the people cut him into several pieces.

You may see the dragon's shape even today, outside the village, though there are some who say it is only a jagged range of mountains.

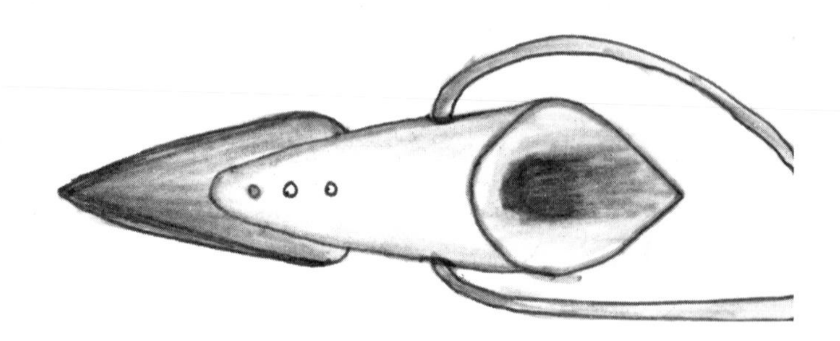

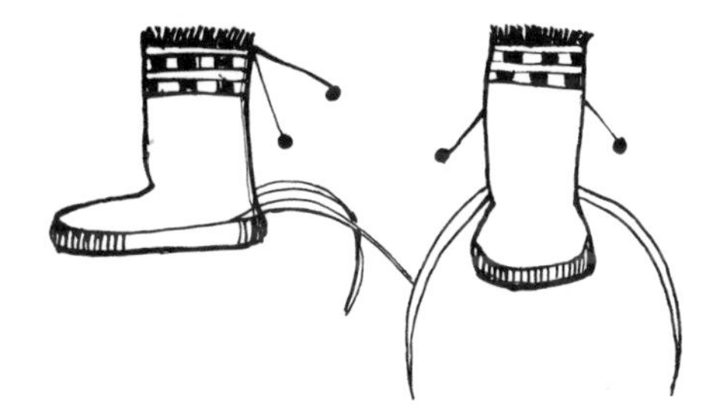

The Flood

LONG AGO, when the heavens were close to the earth, there was a great village with many people. The people who lived in this village were very noisy. The grown-ups danced and sang all night, every night, and slept in the daytime. The children slept at night, and all day, every day, they imitated their elders, and danced and sang loudly.

Since the heavens were so close to the earth, the Chief of the Heavens could get no sleep, day or night, because the people were so noisy. Finally the Chief of the Heavens grew so angry that he decided to punish the people, and he caused the waters to rise in all the rivers, and the tides of the ocean to come up farther and farther on the land.

As the waters rose, the people became frightened. Some got into their big canoes, to escape, and others climbed up on the mountains. Only a few escaped, for the waters kept rising until all the land was covered except the very highest mountain peaks. The people in the canoes drifted for many days.

At last the eagles said, "We will shed our feathers on the waters, and this will be a sign of peace to the Chief of the Heavens. Then perhaps he will cause the waters to go down."

So the eagles began to shed their feathers on the waters, and then the other birds shed their feathers, too, and soon the waters were covered with the downy feathers of the birds.

Then the waters began to go down, and they went lower and lower until they were back where they had been before.

The people came down from the mountains, and out of their canoes, and built new villages. But they had traveled far from the old village, and that is how the many different tribes began.

Ever after, the people knew the magic of the downy feathers of the eagle, and it has always been a sign of peace. Wherever people gathered together the eagle down was held out for all to see, to show that it was a peaceful gathering. In time of war, or arguments, when the chief holds the down of the eagle in his hand and blows it into the air, it is a promise of peace.

The Strong Man

THERE WAS ONCE a great chief who had three nephews. The eldest of these young men was strong and handsome, and the second was hard working and intelligent, but the third and youngest nephew was none of these things, at all! This young man was called Ka-ha-si, and all day, every day, he lay curled up in the ashes beside the fire, and slept. He cared nothing for hunting or fishing, and cared least for work of any kind. The people of the village made fun of Ka-ha-si, and thought that he was low and dirty and a disgrace to the tribe.

But there was something that no one knew about Ka-ha-si, and it was this: Ka-ha-si was the grandson of the Old Man Who Held Up the Earth, and every day the Old Man sent his messenger, the Loon, to instruct the young man as to how to gain great strength.

Each morning, very early, when dawn was just beginning to lighten the skies, and the village was still asleep, Ka-ha-si, following the Loon's directions, would slip quietly from his place by the fire, and disappear into the forest. There he would eat the leaves of the Devil's Club, a magical bush that gave him supernatural strength. Then he would bathe in the ice-cold waters of a certain small stream, for purification. Just before daylight, Ka-ha-si would return to the village, curl up in the ashes, and go to sleep.

A day came when the men of the village made ready to hunt the sea lions. The people depended on the sea lions for most of their meat, but the animals lived on

small rocky islands out in the ocean. To hunt them required great courage, so when the men went down to the water and found Ka-ha-si seated in the canoe, ready to go, they were surprised.

The eldest brother said, "Oh, look who is coming! He who is not strong enough even to lift an oar, let alone hunt the sea lions!"

The second brother said, "Do you think you are a hunter? You, who never even leave the ashes beside the fire?"

Then all the men of the village tried to make Ka-ha-si get out of the canoe, but Ka-ha-si would not move from his place. Finally, the men decided that they would have to let him go with them, and they all got into the big canoe and started out.

As the canoe went farther out to sea, the water grew very stormy and the waves rose higher and higher, breaking across the boat and spraying the men with icy water. But they went on and on, until they came to the islands, great steep-sided rocks that rose straight out of the ocean.

"See how high the waves lift the boat," said the eldest brother to the man at the oars. "Row as close to the rock as you can, and when the wave lifts us up, I will jump out onto the island."

So the men rowed the boat close to the steep side of

the island and when the waves lifted them high up, on a level with the top of the cliff, the eldest brother made a great leap from the boat. With one foot he landed on the rock, but it was wet and slippery, and he lost his balance and fell back into the water. The men pulled him back into the canoe, half drowned.

Then the second brother asked that the canoe be taken close to the rock again so that he could try to leap ashore. Again the boat came close, the waves lifted it high, and the second brother leaped from the canoe, and landed on the island. Now he was face to face with the sea lions—huge creatures with enormous teeth, who came rushing at him, roaring terribly.

The young man jumped away from them, and fell backward into the sea. His friends pulled him, too, from the water, his teeth chattering with cold and fright.

Now Ka-ha-si stood up in the canoe and commanded that he be taken close to shore. The men laughed and scoffed at him, but they thought that it would be good sport to see him fall into the sea, so they took the canoe close to the island. As the waves lifted the boat, Ka-ha-si made a mighty leap, and landed squarely in the midst of the roaring sea lions. Immediately he picked up two of the biggest animals, one in each hand, knocked their heads together, and tossed the bodies

back into the canoe. This he did again and again, until the canoe was so full that the men were afraid that it might sink. Then he leaped back into his place in the boat.

The men pulled at their oars and said not a word during the long trip home. They did not know what to think of Ka-ha-si, and were very ashamed of the way they had made fun of him. Ka-ha-si sat in silence, looking out to sea. When they reached the village, he got out of the canoe and walked up the beach to his hut, where he curled up comfortably in the warm ashes beside the fire.

In the weeks that followed, he continued to stay by the fire, and it was as though nothing had happened at all. The people began to wonder if they had imagined Ka-ha-si's strength and daring on the islands of the sea lions.

Then one day there came a large group of people from another village, and at their head was a tremendous giant. The chief of this tribe stepped forward and said to Ka-ha-si's uncle, "We have come to see if any of your village can equal the strength of our greatest fighter. Bring forth your warriors!"

Now everyone in the village was frightened, because the giant was as big as two ordinary men. Finally, however, the eldest of the chief's three nephews stepped out bravely, and said he would wrestle the giant. The giant laughed, and picking the young man up, tossed him into the snow.

The second of the brothers stepped up, because the pride of the village was at stake. But the giant tossed him aside as he had the first young man. Then the people hid their faces in shame and grief. Their only hope was Ka-ha-si, but he was asleep in the ashes as usual and no one had the nerve to awaken him. They began to wail, while those from the other tribe taunted them. At this moment, Ka-ha-si came out of his hut, yawning and stretching.

"Who is making so much noise?" he demanded. "I can't sleep, for all the noise!"

The giant stepped forward and laughed at him. "Your people are old women," he said. "There is no one strong enough to fight me."

Ka-ha-si looked the giant up and down, and frowned. "I will fight you," he said.

The giant laughed so that the sound was like thunder. "You!" he scoffed. "What can a puny, dirty fellow like you do to me? I will throw you so far you will never come back!"

With that the giant leaned over to pick up Ka-ha-si, but try as he would, he could not lift the young man. It was as though Ka-ha-si's feet were held to the ground by roots. When the giant paused for breath, Ka-ha-si stepped forward, one step, and the ground shook as though a mighty tree had fallen. Then he took another step, and the earth shook again. While the giant stared at him in surprise, Ka-ha-si lifted him in his two hands and threw him to the ground, where he lay moaning and groaning, all the air knocked out of him. His people carried him away, their heads bowed in shame.

Ka-ha-si turned and went back to his warm place beside the fire.

Now the people knew that Ka-ha-si had supernatural strength, and they called after him, "Come back, Ka-ha-si, and we will honor you!"

But Ka-ha-si paid no attention, and when the people looked inside the hut, they found that he was asleep in the ashes.

It was at this time that terrible things began to happen. First, the forest rose against the people, and great trees marched out of their places and into the villages. The men tried to cut them down, but the trees moved always forward, huge and strong, and when one was cut down another took its place. One by one, the villages were destroyed, the people taking to their canoes to escape. When the trees came to the edge of Ka-ha-si's village, the chief told the people to get into the canoes, for the village was being crowded into the sea. As the people were running to and fro, getting their belongings together, Ka-ha-si came out of his hut, blinking at the confusion.

"What is all this?" he asked. "What is going on?"

Then the chief said angrily, "The forest is pushing the village into the sea, and our lives are all in danger. If you would stay awake, you might be of some use!"

Ka-ha-si walked across the village to where the trees were advancing, and began pulling them up by the roots. Tree after tree he pulled up. With these he made a barricade, which he pushed against the forest until the trees had to go back to where they had started and stay there.

When he had finished this, Ka-ha-si went back to his village, and, walking past the rows of silent people, without a word went into his hut.

Next, the mountains began to move slowly down upon the villages. Each time they moved forward, the earth quaked. The people were terrified to see the mountains come closer with every day. Finally the mountains were so close that the people knew they would have to leave in the canoes. Now, as before, Ka-ha-si came out of his hut and asked what the trouble was. The people pointed in panic to the mountains which at that moment came forward again, with a frightful roar and shaking of the earth.

Ka-ha-si stretched out his arms toward the mountains and shouted, "Go back, and never more harm these villages!" Then the mountains fell back, and rivers divided them here and there, so that they never again had power to move.

That night, as Ka-ha-si lay curled in the ashes beside the fire, two strangers came into the village and asked for him. When Ka-ha-si came out, they said, "Your grandfather is old and ill, and cannot much longer hold up the earth. You must come and take his place."

Then the two strangers led Ka-ha-si down to the water where a canoe waited, and they got into the canoe and started out to sea. They had not gone far when a great whirlpool swallowed up the canoe, the two strangers, and Ka-ha-si, and that was the last that the people of the village ever saw of them.

But the Loon came flying back to tell how the whirlpool had taken the canoe to the place under the earth where Ka-ha-si's grandfather was holding up the world, and how Ka-ha-si had taken the burden from the old man, and put it on his own strong shoulders, supporting it carefully with his hands. Ever after, when there was an earthquake, the people knew that Ka-ha-si had changed the position of his feet, or moved his hands, to get a better grip.

Bibliography

BARBEAU, MARIUS: *Haida Myths Illustrated in Argillite Carvings,* Dept. of Resources and Development, National Parks Branch, National Museum of Canada, Ottawa, 1953.

——: *Medicine Men on the North Pacific Coast,* Dept. of Northern Affairs and National Resources, Ottawa, 1958.

——: *Tsimsyan Myths,* Dept. of Northern Affairs and National Resources, Ottawa, 1961.

BILBY, JULIAN W.: *Among Unknown Eskimo,* Seeley Service and Company, Ltd., London, 1923.

BIRKET-SMITH, KAJ: *The Eskimos,* Methuen & Company, Ltd., London, 1959.

BOAS, FRANZ: *Kutenai Tales,* Bureau of American Ethnology, Washington, 1918.

——: *Tsimshian Texts,* Bureau of American Ethnology, Washington, 1902.

——: *Chinook Texts,* Bureau of Ethnology, Washington, 1894.

CARRIGHAR, SALLY: *Moonlight at Midday,* Alfred A. Knopf, New York, 1958.

ESSENE, FRANK J. JR.: *A Comparative Study of Eskimo Mythology,* Ph.D. Dissertation in Anthropology, Graduate Division, University of California, 1947.

Keithahn, Edward L.: *Igloo Tales,* United States Indian Service, 1945.

Powell, J. W.: *Sixth Annual Report of the Bureau of Ethnology,* Bureau of Ethnology, Washington, 1888.

Swanton, John R.: *Haida Texts and Myths,* Bureau of American Ethnology, Washington, 1905.

Rasmussen, Knud: *Intellectual Culture of the Iglulik Eskimos,* Gyldendalske Boghandel, Nordisk Forlag, Copenhagen, 1929.

——: "Caribou Eskimos," *Report of the Thule Expedition,* Vol. VII (Nos. 1, 2, 3),1921–24.

——: *The People of the Polar North, A Record,* Kegan Paul, Trench, Trubner & Co., Ltd., Dryden House, London, 1908.

Rink, Henry: *Tales and Traditions of the Eskimo,* William Blackwood & Sons, Edinburgh and London, 1875.

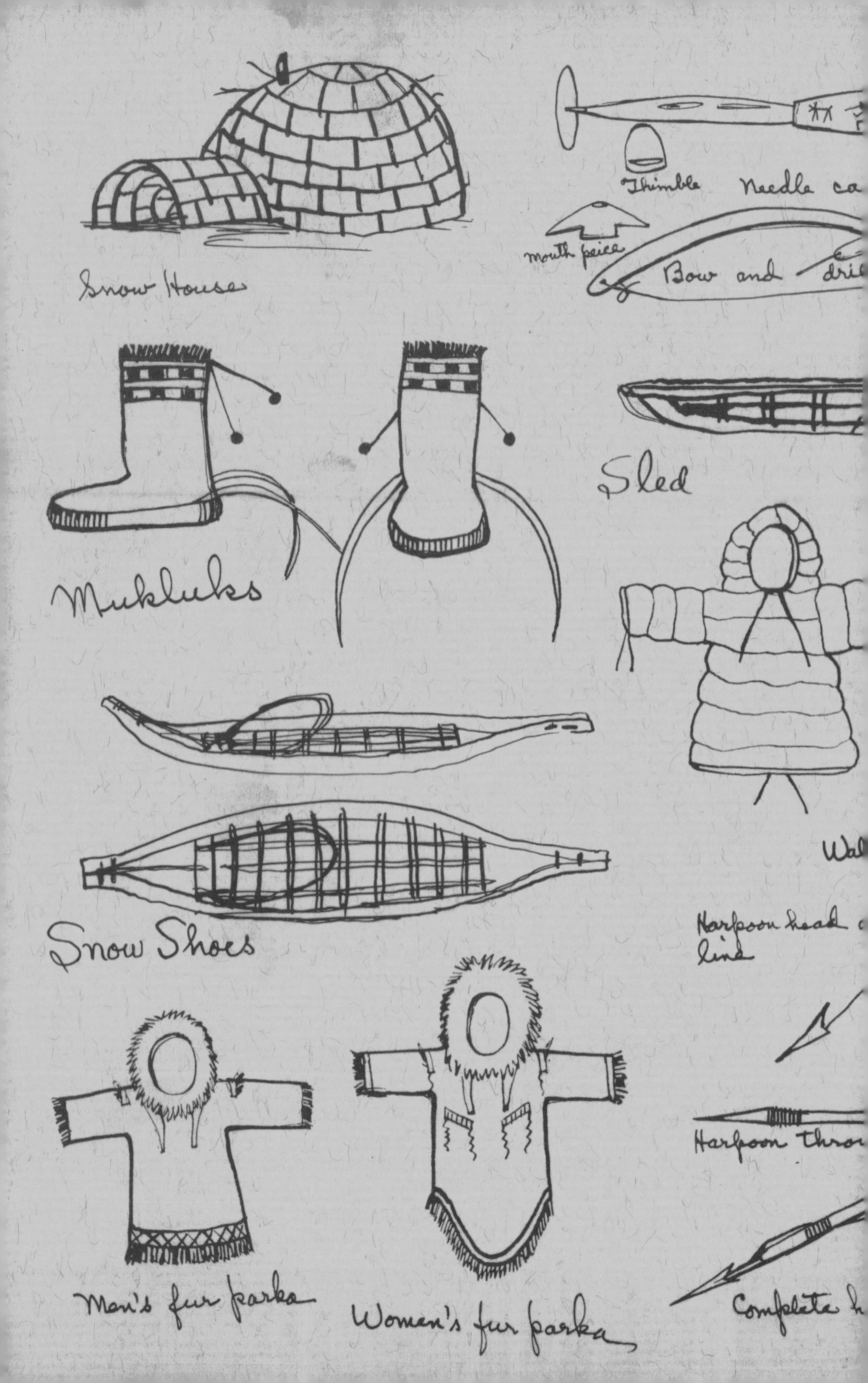
Snow House
Thimble
Needle
mouth peice
Bow and
Sled
Mukluks
Snow Shoes
Harpoon head
line
Harpoon
Complete
Man's fur parka
Women's fur parka